When I Feel Worried

WRITTEN BY

Cornelia Maude Spelman

ILLUSTRATED BY

Kathy Parkinson

Albert Whitman & Company

Chicago, Illinois

For Muriel J. Benz, listening friend—CMS

For my family, especially John, Sarah, and Emily,
with all my love—KP

Books by Cornelia Maude Spelman
After Charlotte's Mom Died • Mama and Daddy Bear's Divorce
Your Body Belongs to You

The Way I Feel Books
When I Care about Others • When I Feel Angry
When I Feel Good about Myself • When I Feel Jealous
When I Feel Sad • When I Feel Scared
When I Feel Worried • When I Miss You

Library of Congress Cataloging-in-Publication Data

Spelman, Cornelia Maude.
When I feel worried / by Cornelia Maude Spelman; illustrated by Kathy Parkinson.
p. cm. — (The way I feel)
Summary: A young guinea pig describes situations that make her worry,
what being worried feels like, and how she can stop worrying.
[1. Worry — Fiction. 2. Guinea pigs — Fiction.]
I. Parkinson, Kathy, ill. II. Title. III. Series.
PZ7.S74727 Wl 2013 [E] — dc23 2013005185

Text copyright © 2013 by Cornelia Maude Spelman
Illustrations copyright © 2013 by Kathy Parkinson
Published in 2013 by Albert Whitman & Company
ISBN 978-0-8075-8895-6

Printed in China
10 9 8 7 6 5 4 3 2 NP 20 19 18 17 16

For more information about Albert Whitman & Company,
visit our web site at www.albertwhitman.com.
Please visit Cornelia at her web site: www.corneliaspelman.com.

Note to Parents and Teachers

Everybody worries. Children worry too. Our worries depend, in part, on our age, but in some ways we all worry about the same things. What will happen? Will someone be there to help me? What will this new situation or these new people be like? Can I do this? Will I perform well? Will this hurt?

These are expectable worries. We adults have additional worries as technology brings instant global news of threats to our safety, severe economic problems, the suffering of others, and acts of violence. These are not worries that children should be expected to manage, and we need to do what we can to reduce their exposure to them.

But how can we best help our young children deal with expectable worries? As always, we have to begin with ourselves. We need to have soothing methods through which we find refreshment and calm so that we can teach them to our children. It can be soothing to be with supportive people, to laugh, play with pets, move our bodies, be in nature, talk and be listened to, enjoy music, sing, read, make art, and watch funny or happy movies or television shows. There are many restorative pleasures available to all of us.

We can develop the habit of noticing good things around us. While it is true that every twenty-four hours has some bad news, each day also has within it examples of help, healing, kindness, support, responsible decision-making, and efforts to improve our world. Paying attention to these good things—even making a list of some positive things about our situation—is more than simply an exercise.

When worries intrude, we can reassure our children that we are there to help them, that we understand their worries, and that we are confident that they will manage each new challenge. Most of all, we can show our children how to use the peaceful and constructive elements in their lives in order to return to a calm place within themselves. Our job is to manage our own worries, and in this way we show them how to manage theirs.

Cornelia Maude Spelman, A.C.S.W., L.C.S.W.

Sometimes I feel worried.

I feel worried when I'm not sure what's happening.

If someone fights or yells, I feel worried.

Sometimes when I am going to do something
I've never done before, I feel worried.

And I feel worried if someone is upset with me.

Worry is a wobbly,
weak feeling.

When I feel worried,
my tummy might hurt.

I don't like
feeling worried.

I want the worry
to go away!

But everyone feels worried sometimes.

When I feel worried, I can tell someone I'm worried.

Someone helps me with my worry.
Someone listens to me or explains what's happening.

Someone holds me.
It helps to have someone hold me.

We talk about good things.

I can make a picture or tell a story
about things I like
that make me happy.

We can listen to music or sing.
Music and singing help me feel better.

I can run and jump and dance.

Moving my body feels good!
It feels good, too, to be outside.

After a while, the weak, wobbly feeling goes away
and I feel better. I laugh.
Laughing helps me feel happy.

When I feel worried,
I know I won't stay worried.

When I feel worried, I know what to do!